The Young Girl's Handbook
of Good Manners

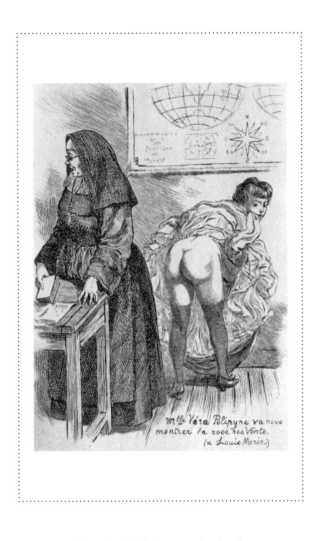

From *La Grande Danse macabre des vifs*
by Martin Van Maele, 1907–08.

THE YOUNG GIRL'S HANDBOOK
OF GOOD MANNERS
for Use in Educational Establishments

Pierre Louÿs

translated by Geoffrey Longnecker

WAKEFIELD PRESS, CAMBRIDGE, MASSACHUSETTS

Wakefield Press, P.O. Box 425645, Cambridge, MA 02142

This book was set in Garamond Premier Pro by Wakefield Press. Printed and bound in the United States of America.

ISBN: 978-0-9841155-1-8

Available through D.A.P./Distributed Art Publishers
75 Broad Street, Suite 630
New York, New York 10004
Tel: (212) 627-1999
Fax: (212) 627-9484

10 9 8 7

Contents

Contents

A FEW YEARS BEFORE winning his early fame, Pierre Louÿs wrote a letter to his brother in which he expressed what had not been an uncommon desire among the Symbolist poets of his generation: "to burn everything before dying, with the satisfaction of knowing that the work will remain virgin, that one will have been the only one to know it as well as create it . . . that it will not have been prostituted."[1]

It is ironic that the body of work that came closest to realizing this ideal for Louÿs, the secret writings he would be best remembered for a century later, would be his sizable production of pornography—etymologically, *pornographos*: the writing of and about prostitutes. After his death, some four hundred kilos (almost nine hundred pounds) of erotic manuscripts were found in his home. If publishing had seemed to him a form of prostitution, his views on prostitution itself had obviously been quite another matter. As his biographer Jean-Paul Goujon puts it, Louÿs in his lifetime had managed to create something of a "Human Comedy of sex."[2] André Pieyre de Mandiargues described him as having been "one of the great and glorious erotomaniacs of the end of the nineteenth century and the beginning of the twentieth,"[3] but even that assessment falls a bit short. Given that all of his unpublished manuscripts were sold at auctions and scattered among collectors after his death, and that a great number of them to this day remain not only unpublished but even unknown, any assessment of Louÿs's erotic work must remain incomplete. One must nevertheless agree with Goujon that Louÿs was, in sheer output if nothing else, "probably the greatest French writer of erotica" there ever was; "only the Venetian Giorgio Baffo could be compared to Louÿs."[4] "Louÿs entered eroticism," Goujon states elsewhere, "the way others enter politics or religion."[5]

Louÿs claimed three vices in his youth: white paper, old books, and dark-haired women. Although he maintained these vices to the end, he engaged in three different vices when deflowering his white paper in his erotic endeavors: young girls, lesbianism, and scatology. It is the first of these three that is most obviously prominent in the present work, the first of his erotic manuscripts that saw publication after his death.

But a more striking theme in much of his erotica (and perhaps nowhere more successfully so than in the present volume) is its prevalent element of parody. If Susan Sontag was correct in claiming that "pornography isn't a form that can parody itself,"[6] Louÿs offered the possibility of its being the ideal genre for parodying everything else—pornography may indeed be the parodic format par excellence. But what is notable about Louÿs's erotic parodies is that his main targets were often his own works: he wrote erotic versions of varying lengths of all his published books, from *Aphrodite* and *The Songs of Bilitis* to *The Adventures of King Pausole* (it would seem that of his main works only *The Woman and the Puppet* escaped having a pornographic double). In this respect, Louÿs's erotica functions as a supplementary universe to his œuvre on more than one level.

This was not the case with his *Handbook*, however, although its model is obvious enough: late nineteenth-century manners are here turned on their head, with ass prominently skyward. The practice and theory of civility that is parodied here has its humanistic roots in Erasmus, who proposed teaching manners and etiquette to boys to help them attain and maintain a noble character. By the end of the nineteenth century, though, such handbooks and educational manuals had become primarily intended for girls, and were little more than a despotic means of regulating sexuality and gender. This is not to say that Louÿs makes for a champion of feminism, or that this handbook (which was not intended for public consumption) was meant as a critique. It is to say, though, that Louÿs adopted a format that at the time was worthy of satire. With its lessons in hypocrisy and admonishments so outrageous they come off more as devious suggestions, his *Handbook of Good Manners* distinguishes itself as one of the few undisputed erotic classics in which (intentional) humor takes precedence over arousal. Although briefly available in a different translation in the early 1970s (as a mass market paperback in Grove Press's Zebra series), it has been widely unavailable in English until now.

Needless to say, this handbook is not recommended for use in educational establishments.

NOTES

1. The letter, dated 16 April 1890, is cited by Jean-Paul Goujon in his magisterial biography, *Pierre Louÿs: une vie secrete* (1870–1925) (Paris: Seghers/J.-J. Pauvert, 1988; new expanded edition: Paris: Fayard, 2002), p. 49.

2. Pierre Louÿs, *L'Œuvre érotique* (Paris: Sortilèges, 1994), p. xxxi.

3. Ibid., p. xix.

4. *Pierre Louÿs*, p. 81.

5. *L'Œuvre érotique*, p. xii.

6. In her essay "The Pornographic Imagination," from *Styles of Radical Will* (New York: Picador, 2002).

THE YOUNG GIRL'S HANDBOOK

OF GOOD MANNERS

GLOSSARY

We have deemed it unnecessary
to explain the words *cunt,*
slit, pussy, snatch, prick, cock, dick,
ball, cum (verb), *cum* (noun),
hard-on, jerk off, suck off, lick,
blow, fuck, screw, lay, frig, bugger,
ejaculate, dildo, lez, dyke,
sixty-nine, going down, quim,
slut, whorehouse.

Every little girl is familiar
with these words.

If you are caught stark naked, put one hand discreetly over your face and the other over your cunt; do not, however, then go on to thumb your nose with the first and jerk off with the second.

Do not pee into the radiator; use the toilet.

Do not hang your dildo at the foot of your bed. Such instruments go under the bolster.

Do not spit on passersby from the balcony—especially if you have cum in your mouth.

Do not pee from the top of the staircase to make waterfalls.

Do not stick a dildo into a little baby's mouth so that it can suck at the milk remaining in the rubber balls, unless you are quite sure that your lez doesn't have syph.

When using a banana, be it for your own amusement or to make the chambermaid cum, do not put said banana back into the fruit bowl without first carefully drying it off.

Do not jerk all your boyfriends off into a pitcher of lemonade, even if you happen to prefer this drink with fresh cum in it. Your dear father's guests might not share your tastes.

If you surreptitiously empty half a bottle of champagne, do not then use it as a pisspot to cover your ass.

Do not suggest that the server should screw a cooked fatted chicken up the ass, without having personally assured that said waiter has no venereal diseases.

Do not do a number two into the chocolate pudding, even if you have lost your dessert privileges and are sure that you won't be eating any of it.

If asked what you wish to drink with your meal, do not reply: "I only drink cum."

Do not slide an asparagus in and out of your mouth while looking languidly at the young man you wish to seduce.

Do not lick a cut apricot while winking at society's most notorious tribade.

Do not use two tangerines to endow a banana with balls.

If you are jerking your neighbor off into his napkin, do it discreetly enough so as not to draw attention.

If your usual lez is seated facing you, do not put on a show of jealousy across the table.

When a grown-up tells a risqué story that children should not understand, do not start letting out inarticulate squeals like a little girl cumming, even if the story should highly arouse you.

If you find a suspicious hair in your soup, do not say: "Look! An ass hair!"

Pierre Louÿs

Do not hide a dildo in the fruit bowl to make the young girls laugh when it is time for dessert.

When you are served bananas, refrain from putting the biggest one into your pocket. This would make the gentlemen smile, and perhaps even the young girls.

If you have yet to reach puberty, do not crush a handful of strawberries between your legs so that you can show everyone that you have your period.

It is in the worst possible taste to slide a dildo under a young girl's napkin in place of her bread roll.

When asking a lady permission to play with her daughter, never say, "I would like her to come." Say, "I would like her to come *over*," which is more proper.

Do not invite your young girlfriends over to go cum-fishing from your dear mother's bidet when you play tea party.

When drawing straws, do not ask a young girl for five or six pubes, especially if you know that she does not even have one.

If you play wet finger, do not wet it between your thighs unless you have complete privacy.

If proposing a game of "show me your prick, I'll show you my cunt," first make sure that grown-ups won't be checking up on you.

The same goes when playing "who can pee the farthest," especially if you are using some little boys as referees.

The same goes if you play "childbirth" with a little porcelain doll in your cunt.

Pierre Louÿs

The same also goes when playing "who can do the dirtiest thing." It may indeed be the favorite game of little girls, but parents never approve of it.

At hot cockles, if you are kneeling before a young man, do not suck his cock; you will be unable to answer the question asked of you.

Putting honey between your legs to get a little dog to lick you is permitted in a pinch; but it is unnecessary to return the favor.

Never masturbate a young man by the window. You never know on whom it might fall.

Do not jump from horseback onto a gentleman for a piggyback ride when you are not wearing fastened pants. If you should be aroused from the ride, you will stain the collar of his frock coat.

To lift one's skirts, sit down on an upright skittle, make it enter you-know-where, and run off with it—holding it solely by means of the "nutcracker" grip—is a most indecent exercise, which no well-raised young girl should imitate, even if she has seen it done with praise from the critics.

If you are playing "whorehouse" with some little girls, do not blacken your belly and thighs to play the role of the Negress.

If you are playing "slut" with some little boys, do not borrow twenty-five crabs from the gardener's daughter so that you can have a true streetwalker's cunt.

When playing hide-and-seek, if you find yourself alone with a young girl in an impenetrable hiding-place, jerk your companion off: it is what is done. And if she makes a fuss, jerk yourself off to encourage her.

If you go horse-riding with a good-looking rider, and if the saddle suddenly fills you with emotion, you may sigh "Ah! . . . ah! . . ." provided you immediately add: "It's for you that I'm doing that, monsieur."

When playing blind man's buff, do not rummage under the skirts of your capture and say that you will recognize her in a moment. This would greatly compromise her.

When someone suggests a game of blind man's buff, do not start acting as if they had said "blind man *in the* buff." Such jokes are facile.

Pierre Louÿs

Do not draw teacher's private parts on the blackboard, especially if she showed them to you in confidence.

After jerking off under your desk, do not wipe your wet finger in your neighbor's hair, unless she asks you to do so.

If you find it more convenient to masturbate in the water closet, simply ask for permission to leave; do not offer your reasons.

If you are asked what planet Uranus is next to, do not reply with "Mycuntus"; and if you are asked what historical figure you would have liked to have met, do not say with a wink: "One of those knights from Cumalot."

These sorts of jokes would make your friends laugh, but not the teacher.

Do not say that the Red Sea got its name because it is shaped like a cunt; nor that Florida is the prick of America; nor that the Jungfrau no longer deserves its name since it has been mounted. These are indeed clever observations, but out of place in a child's mouth.

Do not wet your thumb in your mouth or your cunt when turning a page.

If you are told that man distinguishes himself from the monkey by his upright position, do not protest that he is sometimes unable to maintain that position in bed.

Among the principal verbs of the fourth conjugation, there is no point in citing *to fuck*, I fuck, I fucked, I will fuck, I would fuck, I am fucking, I have fucked. Interesting as the conjugation of this verb may be, you will be scolded more for knowing it than for not knowing it.

If the addition problem that you are given produces the number 69, do not roll about laughing like a little idiot.

If your teacher asks you to take out a pen, do not pretend that you think he is asking you to suck his dick.

In your first-year French class, you will sometimes be given some short naive phrases to translate: "My pussy likes milk. You have a big button. She knew when she was licked. My sister has a nutcracker. She felt a prick. He wanted to come. The hussar got two shots off. He gave her a goose. My brother likes tarts. My father needed a screw."

Do not take it into your head to translate "J'ai un joli petit con. Tu as un gros clito. Elle aime les langues, etc."

Pierre Louÿs

If your teacher brings you to her room and takes you into her arms, extremely agitated, lift your skirts unaffectedly and guide her hesitant hand. You will be relieving her of a great burden.

Do not approach an older student on the first day by asking her if she jerks off. 1. Because the question is pointless: of course she jerks off. 2. Because she may be tempted to lie. Instead, take her secretly to the end of the garden and give yourself over to your little habits. Your example will make her ashamed of her dissimulation.

If one of your elders makes fun of your youth because she has pretty pubes and you are as smooth as a hand, do not call her a hairy bear, Absalom, or a bearded woman: draw instead a lesson from the anger you are feeling and remember to be modest when your own bush is thick.

If the little lock of hair in your locket was cut from the blond pubes on your lezzie's cunt, say instead that they are hairs from someone's head.

Never offer a married woman a dildo, unless she herself has confided her misfortunes to you.

If you offer someone a sliding pencil, refrain from sliding your tongue in a similar manner, or from making the propelling pencil maneuver frenetically in its sheath.

The nicest gift that a little girl can give is her virginity. As that can only be given once, offer the gift of your bottom a hundred times over, and in that manner you will be able to perform a hundred courtesies.

If a girlfriend gives you a ring, put it on the finger you usually use during your voluptuous solitudes. That is a refined expression of appreciation.

If you give an obese penholder to a naive girlfriend, teach her how to utilize it; otherwise it will be a gift wasted.

Rule without exceptions: Never grab the prick of a dancing partner who has not yet gotten a hard-on for you. A quick glance at his pants will dissuade you from making such a blunder.

If you cum while waltzing, say so softly; don't shout it out.

If you see a stain on a young girl's dress, do not ask her if it is cum.

Any partner who puts his prick into your hand intends this gallantry to remain confidential. Do not call everyone over to show what you are holding.

When a gentleman discharges into your hand behind a piece of furniture, it is better to suck your fingers than to ask for a napkin.

A well-raised young girl does not piss into the piano.

If you jerk off in the elevator, put your gloves back on before entering your host's apartment.

When the mistress of the house leans over to kiss you, do not stick your tongue into her mouth. That is not done before witnesses.

Say: "Hello, Madame, how are you?" but never ask a married woman: "Did you have a good fuck last night?" because most often she will have nothing to say.

In a straight-laced salon, never borrow a gentleman's handkerchief to wipe your private parts, even if you are getting wet for him.

If a certain lady visitor pleases you, you may smile at her surreptitiously; but do not wiggle your tongue in your mouth and flash your eyes at her. This would be offering an overly direct expression of a proposition that would be better left implied.

To the person having you admire a rose, do not say: "It looks like Mme X . . .'s cunt." It would indeed be a compliment, but one better saved for a more intimate moment.

If a modest lady tells you: "My son doesn't work as hard as your brother," do not reply: "Yes, but he fucks better." Such praise provides no pleasure to a Christian mother.

If you see a trace of bright red on a young man's moustache, do not ask him in front of everybody: "So Mme X . . . has her period?" An uncomfortable silence would follow.

Never ask a tragedian where she spent her brothel years. Ask her friends.

If you are told that you are a "real tomboy," do not show your cunt to prove the contrary.

To tell a young lady that she has beautiful blond hair is nice; but to ask her aloud whether her pubes are the same color is indiscreet.

If a lady refuses to sit, do not give her advice on the dangers of getting buggered by oafs.

If you are sitting on the corner of a chair, do not move back and forth too much. You will get distracted.

If you notice the gentleman speaking to your mother is beginning to get a hard-on, do not remark on it aloud.

One must always tell the truth; but when your mother is entertaining in the salon and calls you to ask you what you are doing, there is no need to reply: "I'm jerking off, mother," even if it is absolutely true.

Pierre Louÿs

One gets a man by putting a grain of salt on the end of his cock, then sucking the cock until the salt has melted.

Just because Friday is the day of Venus does not mean it has a bad influence on amorous meetings. On the contrary.

If thirteen of you are going to make love on the same bed, do not send your youngest girlfriend to jerk off all alone at the little table. Have the concierge's daughter come up to make fourteen instead.

The same goes if a lover shoots off thirteen times with you in one night: do not let him get up until he has discharged a fourteenth time.

If a young brunette tells you that "Brunettes come into the world through the cunt and blondes through the asshole," you may boldly reply that it is a false rumor. If you are blonde, you may even add a slap.

When you have lost your virginity, do not address Saint Anthony of Padua to get it back. Saint Anthony of the Solitary Retreat has meditated a great deal on sexual questions; but his namesake takes no pleasure in them.

Do not attach a little gold pig to the pubic hairs of your cunt in order to bring luck to what they surround. The gentlemen who tuck your skirts up could laugh at this ensign.

When your parents are receiving, do not drink the bidet water of all the young girls in order to know their thoughts.

When receiving a dildo in the ass, do not demand that the archbishop bless the instrument first. Certain prelates would refuse to do so.

Pierre Louÿs

When a little girl wakes up, she must have completely finished jerking off before beginning her prayers.

If you did not jerk off enough in the morning, do not finish off at mass.

Do not follow service with a copy of *Gamiani*, especially if it is illustrated.

Never tear off your neighbor's pants button when giving to the collection. Do so before entering.

"Anyone who has reason to believe that this marriage should not be, speak now or forever hold your peace," says the priest. But this is just an expression. Do not stand up at these words to reveal secrets.

When you are next to a lady who is kneeling and arching her back, do not ask her whether that position evokes fond memories for her.

At catechism, if the young curate asks you what lust is, do not reply, laughing: "We know better than you!"

On the day of your first communion, if a lady sees you and exclaims: "Isn't she pretty! She looks like a little bride!" do not reply: "All I need is the orange blossom." The retort would be considered disrespectful.

If you suck off a gentleman before receiving communion, be very careful not to swallow the cum: you would no longer have the requisite empty stomach.

When kneeling at the holy table, do not, even in a low voice, invite your little neighbor over to sleep with you that afternoon.

During the sermon, if the preacher seems to believe in the "purity of young Christian girls," refrain from tittering.

If some afternoon you should fuck in a country church, do not wash your sex in the stoup. Far from cleansing your sin, you would on the contrary worsen it.

Pierre Louÿs

If your confessor asks you how many times you have polluted yourself, do not reply: "And you?"

Do not jerk off in the confessional so that you can be absolved immediately after.

When you relate all your filthy things to the good priest listening to you, do not ask him if he is getting a hard-on.

If you go to the confession principal, never ask him to give you his prick so that you can better explain to him what you do with boys; and for that matter, do not show him your cunt so that you can better explain what you do with girls.

If your principal gets in the habit of fucking you, buggering you, or discharging into your mouth, before absolving yourself of all that and everything else, keep him as a lover if you find him good-looking, but find another confessor. From the canonical point of view, the former is inadequate.

Do not climb onto the pedestals of ancient statues to use their virile organs. You should not touch exposed objects, be it with your hand or with your ass.

Do not scribble black curls on the pubes of nude Venuses. If the artist represents the goddess without pubic hair, it is because Venus shaved her bush.

Do not ask the guard why the Hermaphrodite has balls and tits. This question is not his domain.

If you already have boobs, do not expose yourself right and left to give your breast to your doll. That is permitted for wet nurses, but not for little girls.

Do not buy a hoop-stick in order to plant it in your cunt in front of everyone. Do that at home.

Do not walk into urinals just to see the gentlemen piss.

If an old lecher shows you his member at the bend of an alley, you are not the slightest bit obliged to show him your little cunt as an exchange of courtesy.

When you've just fucked in a flowerbed in full daylight, do not wash your ass in the traffic circle pond. That would draw attention.

To give ten sous to a pauper because he has no bread is excellent; but to suck his cock because he has no mistress is going too far; you are under no obligation whatsoever.

If you want to sleep with a gentleman who is passing by, do not ask him yourself. Have your maid talk to him.

Never stuff a garden hose into your private parts. These instruments ejaculate much too strongly and exceed your capacity.

If you notice a violently amorous stallion along the sidewalk, do not reach out to relieve him. That is just not done.

If a mysterious hand comes to feel your ass in a dense crowd, boldly spread your buttocks to facilitate things.

Do not draw pricks on walls, even if you have a real talent as a draftswoman.

Do not suck off gentlemen in street urinals before one in the morning.

If you are getting tongued by a saleswoman in a fitting room at the Louvre, do not yell out that you are coming. It would make for a dreadful scandal.

When exiting the washroom, do not ask for a discount under the pretext that you had only masturbated.

Never enter a whorehouse to ask for a tribade if you do not have twenty francs on you.

If you are a little short when paying for your purchase, do not suggest that you suck the shopkeeper for the rest, especially if his wife is listening.

Do not enter a hairdresser's and shamelessly ask him to curl your cunt hairs.

Do not send your dildo to the notions dealer to have him hang ribbons on it.

Do not put your hand on your neighbor's pants to see if the ballet is giving him a hard-on.

If you notice that a dancer has blond hair and black armpits, do not ask why out loud.

Nor say aloud: "That's the big brunette who sleeps with papa!" Especially if your dear mother is accompanying you.

Even if you have full information as to the talents of the troupe, there is no need to tell everyone in your box: "That one sucks like a pump; she could wear out anyone; and the one on the side likes getting it in the ass."

If you hear some off-color jokes, allusions, or dreadful puns during the play, do not explain them to the grown-ups, even if the grown-ups seem not to be getting them.

Nor ask why the handsome tenor doesn't lay the soprano who keeps singing as if she is all wet for him. Such things are just not done on stage.

Pierre Louÿs

If it is a woman playing the role of the male lover, do not yell out across the theater: "Dirty dyke! Wash your tongue! Where's your dildo?" and other impertinent phrases that the audience would not hear without protest.

When a gentleman is swimming by you, do not grab his balls, however easy his suit makes it for such fondling. Do not jerk off when floating on your back, either, as that could be seen.

When swimming, do not ask those present for permission to pee. Just go ahead and do so.

To whatever degree possible, avoid shutting yourself up in your beach hut with a gentleman. Go in with a young girl instead, as she can go down on you just as well, if not better, and will not compromise you.

If you write obscenities on the walls of your hut, do not sign them with the name of the lady who preceded you.

If you should look through a crack in the planks and see a lady in the next hut over who thinks she is alone and is jerking off, do not knock on the partition to ask her "how it's coming along." Instead of encouraging her, you will disconcert her.

If a gentleman asks you why you are not swimming, do not reply: "I have my period."

Pierre Louÿs

Do not ring for the maître d'hôtel at eleven o'clock at night to ask him for a banana. At that hour, ask for a candle.

Do not ask the hotel manager if the maid knows how to eat pussy. Ask her yourself.

Do not go to the window to call out to passersby, even if you have a great urge to fuck and no one to satisfy you.

You may look through the keyhole to find out why your mama has been holed up the whole day with a young man you do not know, but mind you do not start crying out to her: "Come on, mama! Looking good, looking good!" Instead of exciting her you will bring about a regrettable interruption to her affairs.

If by the same subterfuge you catch a tourist in the act of enjoying himself with a hotel maid in a room, there is no point in crying it out on the stairs to warn the manageress; she certainly could not care less.

Do not utilize the town crier to announce that you have lost your virginity. The man who found it will not be giving it back to you.

If a vagabond should happen to grab you in some deserted locale, let him fuck you right away. It is the surest means to avoid getting raped.

Do not jerk off seven or eight young farmers into a glass to drink the cum with sugar. That would give you a bad reputation in the countryside.

When the gardener waters the ground to make the grass grow, do not water your bush to make your pubes grow. He would laugh at your naiveté.

Get this truth into your head: every person around you, whatever their sex and age, has a secret desire to be sucked by you, but most of them will not dare say so.

Therefore you must start by respecting that human hypocrisy they call *virtue*, and never say to a gentleman in front of fifteen other people: "Show me your prick, I'll show you my slit." He will certainly not show you his prick.

If, on the contrary, you arrange things so as to be completely alone with him, in a spot where he is certain he will not be surprised by anyone, not only will he show you his prick, but he will also have no objections to your sucking it.

The majority of the advice that follows derives from these preceding principles.

If your dear father tells you in a furious voice: "You are no longer my daughter!" do not reply, laughing, "I knew that a long time ago!"

When your dear father appears in society, do not say: "Here's the cuckold!" or, if you must, say it in a low voice.

If you drink a glass of beer in your papa's billiard room, you will be doing wrong; and if you piss into what remains so that no one will notice, you shall only aggravate your misdeed.

When sitting on your dear father's left thigh, do not rub your ass against his prick to make him hard, unless the two of you are alone.

If your dear father asks you to suck him, do not carelessly blurt out that his prick smells like the maid's cunt. He might wonder how you are able to recognize that scent.

Pierre Louÿs

If your dear father takes you to a brothel to have skilled whores eat you out, do not give all those young ladies your address so that you can send each other postcards. A little girl in society must never go to the brothel save in strictest incognito.

If you should be in the midst of jerking off when your father enters your room, stop. It is more proper.

If your dear father sometimes deigns to ejaculate into your little mouth, accept it with eyes lowered, and as if it is a great honor of which you are not worthy. Do not, however, then go brag about it like a little fool to your mama.

Never call your mother: "Old bitch! Pisspot trollop! Whore-licker! Walking pox! etc. . . ." Those are expressions better left to the common herd.

Nor should you ever say to her: "To hell with you! Go fuck yourself! I shit on your face!"

And above all never say to her: "You're a pain in my ass!" Your entry into this world, after all, was what put one in hers.

When your dear mother comes to tuck you in at night, wait until she has left before you start jerking off.

If your dear mother asks you whom you like kissing the most, do not reply: "The maid's cunt."

When you are going to see your lover who is in the habit of buggering you, do not paint your asshole with the lipstick that your dear mother uses for her lips.

Do not strap on a dildo to screw your mother unless she asks you to do so.

Never offer to play a role in your mother's conjugal pleasures, however minor it may be. Wait until she makes the suggestion herself.

There is nothing naughtier than a little girl who sees her brother get a hard-on and does nothing to relieve him.

Jerk your brother off in his bed, never in yours. That would compromise you.

After sucking your brother, do not spit his cum in your governess's face. If she were to complain, there would be trouble.

Most little girls lose their virginity to their brothers, as this offers fewer inconveniences than does the intervention of a stranger.

If your brother mounts you at three o'clock in the morning and kindly plants his prick in your ass, do not respond by saying that you are sleepy.

On the days when your dear sister sees neither her lover nor her tribade, put your hand politely under her skirt and ask her if she would be willing to make do with you.

If she replies that she would prefer to jerk off alone, withdraw quietly.

When your dear sister is in the middle of pissing, do not take the pot away so as to make her piss on the floor; that would be a joke in bad taste.

When she is on her knees in her nightgown, and is saying her evening prayers, only stick your tongue into her ass if she first expresses a desire for you to do so.

If you find a stark naked gentleman in your dear sister's bed, do not go whispering the fact to your father. The visit is not for him.

If your dear sister has pubes on her snatch before you have any yourself, do not tear them out on the pretext that it is unfair.

When your dear sister leaves for the ball, do not write on the back of her white dress: "Please bugger me, gentlemen." Abstain from all inscriptions of this sort.

If your sister is engaged, do not tell your future brother-in-law that she is very talented at sucking dick. Although he will be profiting from this intimate talent, the fiancé would not learn this without a fit of ill humor.

If you are asked what your sister is doing in her room, do not reply that she is jerking off, even if you are sure that it is what she is doing.

Tell no one that your dear sister puts her bolster between her thighs, rubs against it, and calls it Gaston.

If your dear sister helps herself to your dildo several times in a row without giving it back, do not go complain to your parents. Nor should you count on their spirit of justice on those days when she refuses to go down on you. In both cases, you will be whipped.

Do not make fun of your dear sister if she does not want to get buggered. A young girl in society is absolutely free to give only one hole to her lovers.

Pierre Louÿs

When your older sister is in her shift and kneeling on the prayer stool, do not eat her out from behind. That would distract her.

Kneel and say your prayers every evening before jerking off.

Admire the goodness of God who gives every little girl a cunt into which she may plunge any prick in the world, and who, to vary your pleasures, allows you to replace the prick with the tongue, the tongue with the finger, the cunt with the ass, and the ass with the mouth.

Thank him for having created carrots for little girls, bananas for damsels, eggplants for young mothers, and beets for mature ladies.

Thank him for having provided you with the desire to cum and for having created a thousand means to help you do so. If you desire a lover, ask him for one; he shall provide. If it is a lesbian you need, tell him so quite openly. God lies in your heart. You could not deceive him.

Do not pray when you are stark naked. Put on a nightgown and refrain from lifting it in front or behind with others present. If you have a dildo stuffed up your snatch, take it out. The same goes for one in your ass.

Pierre Louÿs

When kneeling to pray, if someone profits from your position and attempts to bugger you, do not lend yourself to such unseemly behavior.

If you suck someone before going to communion, do not swallow the cum, as that would break your fast. You may drink it on Fridays, though. Cum, like milk, is not considered a meat product.

Sometimes an overly supervised young girl will buy a little Virgin of polished ivory and use it as a dildo. This is a usage condemned by the Church.

You may, on the other hand, use a candle to this effect, provided that the candle has not been blessed.

When a little girl has guessed who her mama's sweetheart is, she must not, under any pretext, go tell her papa.

Never tell your mother's lover the name of the young girl who jerks off thinking about him—especially if this young girl is yourself.

If her lover arrives early and your dear mother has you ask him to wait, give him a hard-on, but do not suck him.

When your mother returns from her rendezvous, refrain from asking her if it was good, how many times she did it, if the gentleman had a good hard-on, etc. . . . Such questions would only merit a whipping.

It is equally forbidden to take the beloved aside to ask him: "Did you ejaculate inside her? Is she a dirty little pig? Does she suck nicely? Does she swallow? Does she bugger?" etc. . . .

Above all, do not tell him: "Papa fucked mama last night. My nanny told me so." This information would not be greeted with pleasure.

If you know that your mother is expecting her lover, do not hide under her bed, especially if you intend to jump out and say: "Boo! It's me!" as he is coming in her mouth. You might make her choke.

Nor is this the moment to abruptly enter the room and cry out: "There's papa!" when you know very well that your dear father is away.

If your dear father is absent for six months or a year, do not venture to hide your mother's injector on one of her adulterous days, so that she would only find it too late. The gravest consequences might follow, and the prank would not be enjoyed.

If you discover that you are the daughter of the lover and not the husband, do not call this gentleman "papa" in front of twenty-five other people.

It is your mother's husband that you should call papa. And even if you are certain of having no blood ties to him, do not whisper into his ear: "Now I really *can* suck you: you're not my father!" The end of the sentence would destroy anything truly pleasant about the first words.

If a visitor calls when your mother is making love and you have been asked to answer: "Mama is unwell," do not provide details as to her illness. If you are asked: "What seems to be the matter?" do not reply: "A prick in the ass."

Pierre Louÿs

It is not proper for a little girl to still be a virgin after the age of eight, even if she has been sucking cock for several years.

Once you have turned eight, if someone asks you for your virginity, you must give it; if it is not asked for, you must offer it politely.

To lose your virginity, lie down in the middle of the bed, remove your shift or at least lift it up to your armpits, spread your legs apart and open the lips of your cunt with both hands. If the gentleman prefers to first deflower your little buttocks, present them at once: it is up to him to decide which path pleases him most.

If you lose your virginity on the grass, or on a garden bench, or in a carriage, or on a toilet seat, or in the cellar, on a barrel, or in the attic on an old crate, do not complain of having been badly screwed. One fucks where one can.

Once you have lost your virginity, be wary of telling your dear father. That is not done.

Do not even tell your nanny unless she is in the habit of jerking you off every evening, in which case she is likely to discover the wolf's tracks herself.

Have all the lovers you want, but do not tell the young ones what you do with the old ones. Or vice versa.

Never forget to say "please" when you ask for a prick, or to reply "thank you" when you are given one.

When you are standing before a gentleman with a hard-on at the level of your waist and he intends to frig you, climb onto a stool so that your little cunt may rise to the occasion.

In general, though, it is better to kneel on an armchair, lift your skirts onto your back, and open your buttocks with both hands in such a way as to present your two orifices, between which the gentleman will be able to choose his way freely. This is the prettiest position.

After sucking someone, do not go to the kitchen to spit the cum into the cooking pot. The staff would not think well of you.

If your dear mother accompanies you to your lover's, let her fuck him first: that is the way things are done. And when you yourself are fucking, eat her out to keep her occupied.

As long as you have not reached the age of puberty, there is no danger in making love to Negroes if Negroes excite you; but as soon as you get your period, ask your black lovers to bugger you, for if you give birth to a little mulatto, it would be sure to hurt your reputation.

Pierre Louÿs

If you are a little girl who is always at it, and if your shirt is always full of cum and your sheets covered in stains, jerk the maid off a little so that she does not say anything.

Never suck a manservant when the cook is around. She would get jealous and expose you.

When getting into your parent's automobile, do not kiss the chauffeur on the neck, even if you are very grateful for his having just fucked you six times over.

Do not complain to your dear mother that the new maid does not want to eat you out. Have her dismissed under another pretext.

Do not aggressively bugger the chambermaid with a broom handle. You might really hurt her.

When your English maid is asleep, do not cut her pubes so that you can make blonde mustaches for yourself.

If the cook really wants to let you examine her cunny in all its details, do not stuff it with itching powder.

If you catch the kitchen maid jerking off with the rolling pin, do not repeat this to your dear mother. When a poor girl is in heat, she takes what she has at hand.

Rim jobs are not appropriate things to give to your domestics. This is a service that you may ask from them, but one less proper to render.

Never enter the staff dining quarters, lift your skirts up to your waist, and cry out: "Now everyone screw me!" These people would lose all respect for you.

Whatever the venality may be of the manservant whom you are screwing, do not give him one of your dear mother's jewels every time he mounts you.

Do not demand that the chambermaid eat you out more than twice a day. One must not overwork the staff.

Pierre Louÿs

Called on with the honor to recite a compliment before the President of the Republic, do not whisper into his ear when he kisses you: "Come to mama's, I'll get you hard."

If you recognize him as an old regular customer of the brothel where you prostitute your little mouth, do not call him "big baby" before his military cabinet.

Nor call him "old lecher" and blackmail him for one hundred thousand francs in exchange for your discretion.

If, on the other hand, he secretly abducts you and plunges at your behind to satisfy his lechery, you are under no obligation to be raped by the Chief of State.

If you willingly sleep with him and he asks you to go wee wee into his mouth, do not object that this act would be unworthy of the respect you owe him. He knows protocol better than you.

You can ask the President of the Republic for a lock of his hair to remind you of his favors, but it would be indiscreet to cut off his prick as a memento.

If, in the course of a nocturnal ramble, you run into the President of the Republic completely drunk and lying in the gutter, have him taken to the Élysée with the honors due his title.

If the President of the Republic suddenly dies as you are sucking his cum, you may recount the story to everyone: you will not be prosecuted. There are precedents.

Never ask a gentleman: "Do you need a suck?" That is how little streetwalkers express themselves. Say in a low voice, and in his ear: "Would you like my mouth?"

If he is a gentleman whom you have not previously sucked, do not start in by skillfully licking up and down his prick and behind his balls. He would form a bad opinion as to your past.

Take his prick into your mouth modestly, lowering your eyes. Suck slowly. Spread your jaws apart so as not to bite and clench your lips so as not to drool.

When the gentleman is about to cum, do not interrupt yourself to ask him how his mother is doing, even if you had forgotten to do so before.

When he ejaculates, silently swallow it all to the very last drop and then say something nice about the taste of the liquor you just drank.

Having done that, do not ask the gentleman to give you ten sous. Little society girls suck for the honor.

If you have slept with a gentleman whom you know very well and whom you have made ejaculate twenty times over, you may then go ahead and suck his balls and stick your tongue into his ass by way of a prelude; but let him think that he is the only one to whom you have granted these small kindnesses. If the gentleman goes limp between your lips, blame not the weakness of his powers, but your own inexperience.

If he should die, rebutton his pants before you call the maid, and never tell anyone under what circumstances he rendered his soul unto God.

Pierre Louÿs

As soon as you have gotten into bed with a friend, put your hand on her cunt; do not wait for her to ask you.

Do not make fun of a young girl because she is still a virgin. Some girls are unfortunate enough to have never gotten anyone hard.

Remember that in the position known as "69," the place of honor is reserved for the person lying down. A little girl should always take the place on top.

If your friend should work her tongue clumsily over the spot where she is touching you, it would be in the worst possible taste to piss in her face in a fit of annoyance.

When you turn out the light and say to your companion: "Let me call you Arthur," do not hide the fact that you are confiding in her.

Do not make a young girl who has just executed a most skillful rimming over your asshole feel ashamed. She certainly did it with the best intentions.

If a reversal of fortune obliges your parents to prostitute you before the legal age, prove yourself worthy of the confidence they have accorded you and prove to them that they were not wrong to vaunt your young talents.

When shut up with an old man, avoid undressing right away. Let him grope about under your skirts and slide his venerable fingers over to the part of your body that interests him most.

Do not abuse honorary titles when speaking to your guardian. "Excellency," "Your Grace," and "Mr. Vice President of the Senate" are expressions best left aside. Moreover, do not be afraid to call him: "Pig!" "Little bastard!" "You big saucy devil!" Such coarse words, if pronounced with a little smile, are always well received.

Turning one's back to an old man under any circumstance is considered most impolite. A naked little girl who presents her buttocks to a dirty old man, however, is sure not to be scolded.

If the gentleman asks you any questions regarding your habits, try to describe them as being worse than they are. Assert, for example, that you masturbate four or five times a day, even if you normally only do so once, and that you lick your dear mother's clitoris every evening, even if you know quite well that she prefers your lover to do so.

DO NOT SAY: "My cunt."
SAY: "My heart."

DO NOT SAY: "I want to fuck."
SAY: "I'm tense."

DO NOT SAY: "I just came like crazy."
SAY: "I feel a little tired."

DO NOT SAY: "I'm going to jerk off."
SAY: "I'll be right back."

DO NOT SAY: "When I have hair on my cunt."
SAY: "When I am grown up."

DO NOT SAY: "I prefer tongues to cocks."
SAY: "I only like refined pleasures."

DO NOT SAY: "I only drink cum between meals."
SAY: "I'm on a special diet."

DO NOT SAY: "I have twelve dildos in my drawer."
SAY: "I never get bored when I'm alone."

DO NOT SAY: "Decent novels bore me to death."
SAY: "I would like something interesting to read."

DO NOT SAY: "She comes like a mare pissing."
SAY: "She's a hothead."

DO NOT SAY: "When you show her a prick, she gets angry."
SAY: "She's eccentric."

DO NOT SAY: "She'd rather jerk off than eat."
SAY: "She's a sentimental girl."

DO NOT SAY: "She's the biggest whore on earth."
SAY: "She's the greatest girl in the world."

DO NOT SAY: "She lets anyone who goes down on her bugger her."
SAY: "She's a bit of a flirt."

DO NOT SAY: "She's a raging lesbian."
SAY: "She's not at all flirtatious."

DO NOT SAY: "I saw her get fucked up both holes."
SAY: "She's an eclectic girl."

DO NOT SAY: "He's hung like a horse."
SAY: "He's an accomplished young man."

DO NOT SAY: "His prick is too fat for my mouth."
SAY: "I feel like a little girl when I talk to him."

DO NOT SAY: "He came on my face and I on his."
SAY: "We made an impression on each other."

DO NOT SAY: "When you suck him, he shoots his load right away."
SAY: "He's impulsive."

DO NOT SAY: "He gets off three times without withdrawing."
SAY: "He has a very firm character."

DO NOT SAY: "He fucks little girls very well, but he doesn't know how to bugger them."
SAY: "He's a simpleton."

Refrain from off-color comparisons.

DO NOT SAY: "Hard as a prick, round as an anus, wet as my slit, as salty as cum, no bigger than my little button," and other expressions not admitted into the Academy's dictionary.